clever
little
WITCH

For Olive

—M. T. V.

To Gena and Yuna

—H. Y.

MARGARET K. McELDERRY BOOKS
An imprint of Simon & Schuster Children's Publishing Division
1230 Avenue of the Americas, New York, New York 10020
Text copyright © 2019 by Muon Van
Illustrations copyright © 2019 by Hyewon Yum
MARGARET K. McELDERRY BOOKS is a trademark of Simon & Schuster, Inc.
For information about special discounts for bulk purchases, please contact Simon & Schuster
Special Sales at 1-866-506-1949 or business@simonandschuster.com.
The Simon & Schuster Speakers Bureau can bring authors to your live event. For more
information or to book an event, contact the Simon & Schuster Speakers Bureau
at 1-866-248-3049 or visit our website at www.simonspeakers.com.
Book design by Semadar Megged • The text for this book was set in StellarClassicSG.
The illustrations for this book were rendered in Acrylic Gouache and color pencils.
Manufactured in China • 0519 SCP
First Edition 10 9 8 7 6 5 4 3 2 1
Library of Congress Cataloging-in-Publication Data
Names: Van, Muon, author. | Yum, Hyewon, illustrator.
Title: Clever little witch / Muon Thi Văn; illustrated by Hyewon Yum.
Description: First edition. | New York : Margaret K. McElderry Books, [2019] |
Summary: Little Linh, the cleverest witch on Mãi Mãi Island, has everything she needs plus
an impossible little brother, Baby Phu, and she will do anything to get rid of him.
Identifiers: LCCN 2018024752 (print) | ISBN 9781481481717 (hardcover) | ISBN 9781481481724 (eBook)
Subjects: | CYAC: Babies—Fiction. | Brothers and sisters—Fiction. | Witches—Fiction.
Classification: LCC PZ7.1.V35 Cle 2019 (print) | DDC [E]—dc23
LC record available at https://lccn.loc.gov/2018024752

clever little WITCH

muon thị văn
hyewon yum

MARGARET K. McELDERRY BOOKS
New York • London • Toronto
Sydney • New Delhi

I'm Little Linh,
the cleverest little witch
on Mãi Mãi Island.

Do you know what every
clever little witch needs?

One: a trusty broomstick.

Two: a well-worn
book of powerful spells.

Three: a rare and magical pet.

Do you know what a clever
little witch does not need?

A baby brother.

A baby brother will ride your broomstick
without permission and cry when he falls off.

A baby brother will eat pages
from your spell book and spit them
up on your favorite cloak.

A baby brother will use your mouse as a flashlight
and keep you awake for hours.

I do not like Baby Phu one bit.

I offered Baby Phu to the troll beneath the bridge, but he said, "Thanks, but no thanks." The last baby brother gave him hiccups for a week.

I offered Baby Phu to the forest fairy queen,
but she said, "No way!"
   She liked using baby's breath in her potions, but dirty
diapers made her sneeze like crazy.

I even offered Baby Phu to the Orphanage for Lost and Magical Creatures, but they returned him right away. The werewolves could not sleep with him around.

If I can't give my brother away, then I'll keep him.
After I change him into something nicer. Like a goldfish.

I got out my big book of spells.

"Gold bars . . . gold earrings . . . gold fish— Oh, no!"
Baby Phu had eaten half the spell.
Still, I'm the cleverest little witch on Mãi Mãi Island.
I can guess what the other half is.

I aimed my wand at my brother and said, "From the tip of your nose to the top of your toes, bubble eyes, marble size, let me see those fishy eyes!"

But something went terribly wrong.
Baby Phu didn't become a goldfish.
   He became a frog. A croaking frog that
hopped onto the table and spilled potion
everywhere.

"Let's try this again. From the tip of your nose to the top of your toes, splashy flips, puckered lips, let me hear those fishy sips!"

But something went terribly wrong.
Baby Phu didn't become a goldfish.
He became a seal. A barking seal that knocked
over the crystal ball and chased my mouse.
I tried one more time.

"From the tip of your nose to the top of your toes,
slippery wriggle, scaly jiggle, let me feel that fishy wiggle!"

But something went terribly, terribly wrong.
Baby Phu didn't become a goldfish.
He became a dragon.
A huge, scowling dragon that stole my wand.

I jumped on my broom and flew after it.

The dragon's tail smacked my broom.
The broom wobbled.
The broom zigzagged.
I was going to fall!

"Help!"

There was a loud crash.
The broom lay on the ground.

But not me.

The dragon had grabbed me right
before the broom hit the ground.

The dragon put me down gently.

Then it did something amazing.
It changed into my baby brother.
"Witch's pigtails!" I said. "How did you do that?"

I'm lucky to have a baby brother.

Right?